THE ANCHORAGE

Poems

Mark Wunderlich (signature)

Mark Wunderlich

University of Massachusetts Press   Amherst

Copyright © 1999 by
Mark Wunderlich
Printed in the United States of America
LC 98-53493
ISBN 1-55849-200-3
Set in Granjon
Printed and bound by BookCrafters, Inc.

Library of Congress Cataloging-in-Publication Data

Wunderlich, Mark, 1968–
    The anchorage : poems / Mark Wunderlich.
        p.   cm.
    ISBN 1-55849-200-3 (cloth : alk. paper)
    1. Gay men—Poetry. I Title.
PS3573.U46A8   1999
811' .54—dc21   98-53493
                                                       CIP

British Library Cataloguing in Publication data are available.

for Allan

Between my Country—and the Others—
There is a Sea—
—Emily Dickinson

ACKNOWLEDGMENTS

Grateful acknowledgment is made to the editors of the following publications in which some of these poems have appeared:

Agni Review:	Hunt
Boston Review:	Through an Opening Door, From a Vacant House
Chelsea:	Unmade Bed; Chapel of the Miraculous Medal; Fourteen Things We're Allowed to Bring to the Underworld; Letter Written to a Verse by Karen Carpenter; No Place Like Home; All That, Stammering
Cortland Review:	Predictions About a Black Car; This Heat, These Human Forms
GW Review:	The Shot
Graham House Review:	Pale Notion; Thirst
Harvard Review:	Peonies
Paris Review:	Take Good Care of Yourself; Suture
Poetry:	On Opening (1995); To Sleep in a New City (1995); In the Winter of This Climate (1995); Aubade (1996). Copyright Modern Poetry Association, 1995, 1996
Quarterly West:	Given in Person Only; Continent's Edge; The Anchorage; Cease, the Heart is With Me; The Mare
Rhetoric Review:	Winter of Heaven, Winter of Ash (first published as "Snow").
Southwest Review:	One Explanation of Beauty
Yale Review:	How I Was Told and Not Told; The Bruise of This

"Take Good Care of Yourself" also appeared in *Night Out: Poems about Hotels, Motels, Bars and Restaurants* (Milkweed Editions, 1997).

"The Bruise of This" and "How I Was Told and Not Told" also appeared in *Things Shaped in Passing: More "Poets for Life" Writing from the AIDS Pandemic* (Persea, 1996).

"Aubade" also appeared in the *1995/1996 Anthology of Magazine Verse and Yearbook of American Poetry.*

Many thanks to the University of Arizona Poetry Center, the Fine Arts Work Center of Provincetown, and the Wallace Stegner Fellowship Program of Stanford University for the gifts of refuge and support. Also, special thanks to Mary Jo Bang, Sarah Blake, Caroline Crumpacker, Sally Dawidoff, Timothy Donnelly, Sarah Messer, and Claudia Rankine for their help in shaping many of these poems.

To my teachers Lise Goett, J. D. McClatchy, and Lucie Brock-Broido my appreciation and gratitude.

And to my family, my love and thanks for their encouragement.

CONTENTS

I.

II.

III.

I.

Take Good Care of Yourself

On the runway at the Roxy, the drag queen
fans herself gently, but with purpose.
She is an Asian princess, an elaborate wig
jangling like bells on a Shinto temple,
shoulders broad as my father's. With a flick

of her fan she covers her face, a whole
world of authority in that one gesture,
a screen sliding back, all black lacquer
and soprano laugh. The music in this place
echoes with the whip-crack of 2,000

men's libidos, and the one bitter pill
of X-tasy dissolving on my tongue is the perfect
slender measure of the holy ghost,
the vibe crawling my spine exactly,
I assure myself, what I've always wanted.

It is 1992. There is no *you* yet for me
to address, just simple imperative. *Give
me more. Give.* It is a vision, I'm sure
of this, of what heaven might provide—a sea
of men all muscle, white briefs and pearls,

of kilts cut too short for Catholic girls
or a Highland fling. Don't bother with chat
just yet. I've stripped and checked my shirt
at the door. I need a drink, a light, someplace
a little cooler, just for a minute, to chill.

There is no place like the unbearable ribbon
of highway that cuts the Midwest into two unequal
halves, a pale sun glowing like the fire
of one last cigarette. It is the prairie
I'm scared of, barreling off in all directions

flat as its inhabitants' A's and O's. I left
Wisconsin's well-tempered rooms
and snow-fields white and vacant as a bed
I wish I'd never slept in. Winters
I stared out the bus window through frost

at an icy template of what the world offered up—
the moon's tin cup of romance and a beauty,
that if held too long to the body
would melt. If I felt anything for you then
it was mere, the flicker of possibility

a quickening of the pulse when I imagined
a future, not here but elsewhere, the sky
not yawning out, but hemmed in. In her dress
the drag is all glitter and perfect grace,
pure artifice, beating her fan, injuring

the smoky air, and in the club, I'm still
imagining. The stacks of speakers burn
and throb, whole cities of sound bear down
on us. I'm dancing with men all around me,
moving every muscle I can, the woman's voice

mixed and extended to a gorgeous black note
in a song that only now can I remember—
one familiar flat stretch, one wide-open vista
and a rhythm married to words
for what we still had to lose.

Given in Person Only

Tompkins Square Park's a mess of shopping carts
overflowing with what's been cast off,
and pierced and tattooed punks affecting poses
soon grown into, arms speckling with tracks,
so when a girl extends a blue-nailed hand
I press to her palm the dollar she requests,

not because it will do her, or me, a bit
of good, but because today I am willing
to give myself to anyone, should they ask.
I've just come back from the clinic,
its waiting room a jumble of secondhand plaid
where Lupita drew blood from a forearm's vein

she called *the kind she likes to see.*
Before her on the gunmetal desk
was the blueprint questionnaire mapping
my sexual history, the penciled dots
a constellation of what I wanted and what
I got. I know I've spent too much time

leaning against walls in bars, chewing ice
from an overpriced drink while shielding an ear
from some techno beat, the bass vibration
in the rib cage the sound desire makes.
There have been back rooms where
I didn't know to whom the hands belonged

or how many, pure surrender. Then
there were the ones *with* names—
the man who bicycled through the snow,
stood in my living room and cried,
our bodies laboring to extinguish
some common flame, or the one

whose shirts still hang in my closet, limp torsos
washed out with use. I don't regret
the hunger that drove me to dark rooms,
stairwells, steam rooms or beaches,
park benches, parked cars, locker rooms
or clubs—locations that give shape

to my notion that sex is like faith—
at its center, it is always the same, unwavering.
I won't apologize for the want and urge,
veiled in daylight as a curtain hides a stage,
no matter what Lupita will have for me
when she splits open her envelope's

folded white wings. In Chelsea the boys skate,
shirtless in late summer, brown thighs
and unflinching faces rolling by like gods.
It's muggy again, the way Manhattan
always seems in my dreams, and above
the water towers and angled roofs, the sun

insists on disrobing through the clouds.
I'll remake myself once again, shed
rapture and sweet release, and replace it
with something equally consummate and strange.
So let the city do as it must and break us down
to dust and skeletons. I'm just beginning.

The Trick

I made love with a man—hugely muscled, lean—the body
I always wished for myself. He kept pulling my arms
up over my head, pinning them there, pressing me down

with his entire weight, grinding into me roughly,
but then asked, begged, in a whisper of such sweetness,
Please kiss me. Earlier that evening, he told me

he'd watched a program about lions, admired
how they took their prey—menacing the herds at the water hole
before choosing the misfit, the broken one.

What surprised him was the wildebeests' calm
after the calf had been downed, how they returned to their grazing
with a dumb switching of tails. Nearby the lions looked up

from their meal, eyed the hopping storks and vultures,
before burying their faces, again, in the bloody ribs.
As a teenager, I wished to be consumed,

to be pressed into oblivion by a big forceful man.
It never happened. Instead I denied myself nourishment—
each unfilled plate staring back satisfied me, deprivation

reduced to a kind of bliss I could lie down in
where I remained unmoved, untouched.
Early on I was taught that the body was a cage,

that illness was a battle fought with chaos,
the viruses themselves unnatural; that sex lived
in some pastel chamber that gave way to infants,

first cousins, the handing down of names.
No one ever mentioned being taken in the dark,
or wanting to be broken open, pushed beyond words,

tongue thickening in another human mouth,
or how a person could be humiliated and like it.
To my surprise, I found myself struggling under this man,

pushing my chest up against his chest, arms straining
against the bed, until some younger, hungrier
version of myself lay back on top of me and took it—

the heaving back, the beard, the teeth at the throat.

Through an Opening Door

On Fourteenth Street, the vendors push
their ragged brooms and sweep each bottle's
empty headache into the gutter and wash it
away. Blocks west of here last night,
a drag queen of unfailing commitment strode
up Eighth Avenue, arm raised to hail a cab,

leather coat splayed out behind, oily wings.
It was 4 A.M., the tender hour, when the boys
in the bars, paired off or spent, slink home
to sleep off chemical bliss, my own hours
of recovery moving toward me like a slow blue
bus. In daylight, you'd not recognize it,

this place—the meat packers, the Spanish
speakers hunting frothy buttermint dresses
hung from delicate hooks behind glass, plastic
shoes, reptilian imitations, nosing out
from racks on the street. You'd not imagine
the back-room frenzy of the night, the boy bent

on getting me off, his mouth a dark harbor,
his eyes rolled upward, two blue beads.
In the morning I'll recall only a bit of this,
the way the blue beads from the necklace recall
the neck, the hair's hanging drape, these
nights all about the blurring of detail,

but no chemical can better history, free
this bit of you hooked into me like a stitch,
or blur this scene played out in the shut box
of my heart—you rising up from the bed,
toward a new beginning, through an opening door.
The drag on the avenue can't get a cab,

her fear and the driver's suspicion speeding
in opposite directions, face fallen, ankles
turned slightly outward in their heels, leather
underthings concealing just enough to keep
everyone curious, who turns toward me as I watch
and says, *Baby, you just give yourself away.*

Continent's Edge

The surf washed up its rows of green
and the debris scattered its fractured narrative—

a woman's shoe, purple ribbons, a gull's
battered carcass, countless plastic bags, and nets

the clammers use to cart home what their spades turn up,
the hollow shells of trilobites, the crusted thorax of a crab—

all of it rinsed and tilted landward to the beach.
Up the sand crest of dune along trampled paths

are the dished clearings worn of sawgrass
where humans pressed themselves against each other.

Left behind are the telltale markers—
empty tubes of lubricant, the flaccid sacks of condoms

and their silvery wrappers, fluttering tissues gummed with sand.
Once on West Street, where the Hudson grinds out to sea

I watched the she-males flock the cobblestones,
all feathers and leatherette, sequins and razor stubble,

stepping up to slow-turned car windows. I am secretly in league
with them—their nocturnal ministering and bodily commerce,

though there's no ignoring how a car's dark interior
could compromise their tenuous elegance. Somewhere

between the clavicle's arc and swell of calf these givers
offer the succor of mouths and hands, the john's forward thrust

piercing gender's blur and entering the shadowy inner circle
pleasure casts like the compass of the sling-back's spike heel.

Through the lace's confusion, corset stays
and the zipper's small teeth, sex offers up

its one heedless moment, some bifurcated taste
compelling a man to want a man who looks like a woman,

a scaffold of artifice separating desire
from the shaved and perfumed figure beneath the dress.

I have learned to appreciate a man's muscles
for their individuation, carved and unsubtle as reliefs

of Greek soldiers naked and locked in a symmetrical war.
Bound to this musculature is my wish to see myself

in the man I am with, albeit a new version—
the crude tattoo I never allowed, the uncut organ

or unlined face. Maybe the johns want
a man gentler or more graceful than they know themselves

to be, the exchange making possible
the well-appointed rooms of the imagination, just as I

want someone powerful enough to pin me to myself for a while.
Here among the dunes and sexual debris, the waves

give me nothing but what's done for,
the sand shifting with each wave's assault,

sometimes gentle, sometimes hard, the way a hand
draws back an undone shirt.

Cease, the Heart is With Me

Today I've felt it, like bees humming, wanted the mean
pleasure-taking muscle of you, wished for that familiar spiral
to my most greedy self, but instead I turn to pornography,

take a magazine from the drawer and open to a young man—
handsome, in the conventional manner, body waxed,
face a mask of bronzer. He is climaxing. Others in the room

are filming it, tilted lights illuminate the beatific look
on his face. It seems he has forgotten his troubled ego,
onlookers, the camera's unblinking eye and for a moment

sees no one, is not even there, but is released the way a razor
severs hair from the human head. On a postcard taped to my wall
the marbeline torso of St. Sebastian bends to an executioner's will,

reliving the ecstasy of arrow piercing pectoral and triceps.
His groin is a complicated knot, eyes upward in petition,
and already a halo rings him with its celestial shield,

breaking death's normality and guaranteeing ascent
through the sky's pressure of blue. Both are text, men of paper,
one pushing a T-shirt up in a fit, the other with arms too long

and narrow feet that could never support his weight.
The painting's owner surely noticed the soldier's muscular
abdomen and outstretched neck, unblemished skin reflecting

an inner reservoir of faith. The column to his right crumbles
the way Rome crumbled, an empire's noble intentions
lanced from within, the martyr more beautiful for being unreal.

In the background the executioners flee on foot, a mask of amusement
stretched across their faces, the seed pod of cruelty
blooming in the shadow of their hearts, retreating

from the narrow sliver of grace offered up to the lens
whose job it is to take it all in, to forgive everything—
a young man's spilled semen, arrows piercing flesh.

The Anchorage

I think you would like this seaside town—it makes me dream of
    whales.
All night they break through the dark, unhinging monstrous jaws,

their flukes stirring the surface to an oily calm
while gulls swoop to pull the krill from the great open maw

and all day I've been thinking of the twelfth-century postulant
sealed as a child in the monastery wall, sealed with her anchor.

Together the women sang the canticles, opening
only for the priest's bony finger touching the sacrament

to their lips, then the sour sponge of Christ's blood, kissed
back. Years ago, I walked an overgrown road through the woods

where bees turned treble arcs in a haze of goldenrod
and rusting hulks of implements leached red on the ground.

There the white came in. It came in to flood my brain,
and if I did not know it was vascular, I'd swear

it was some facsimile of heaven—seven platinum spheres rotating
over shifting tiles, then a veil hemmed in ten thousand stitches

of light, the pain a toll for foresight's privilege.
And in the migraine's aftermath, the glass lid lifted up,

the doves whistling plaintive as ghosts, this is when
flesh married suffering in the mind. Above my bed

I still have the picture of the Virgin Mary—tender feet
braced on a crescent moon's gold hooks, a cape

spilling with roses, desert-rare and pungent
as the flowering vines crawling my own house's window,

where I would sit sealed behind the shut lids of the blinds,
hidden from a cold-shocked sky, thinking how a body satisfies.

I've moved six times since then, farther from that northern lake's
glass eye, with its cataracts of fish shacks,

the tar-paper house where laundry webbed the shrubs,
cats coiled in window wells, the mop water

freezing on the floors and my breath clouding as I crept
the stairs to my room. Here at the shore, I still live

with the threat of seizure, but fear it not as much,
heaven less my childhood vision of a bleached and rotating city

than a rocking and viscous zone of slow-moving figures,
our shadows sealed together, opening only for the holiest suste-
    nance.

There will be no blood there, no virus linking up its cellular chains
to consume the flesh, no houses remembered for the shapes

that move through them. Just motion, and union, and light.

From a Vacant House

It is hard to want a thing you know will hurt another,
yet the heart persists, doesn't it, with its dark urges, liquid wish?

A sea town. Gulls, those malefica, uselessly scissor
thin-boned bodies against a beach washed of its will,

where a season ago women lay, dogs and children fastened
to the long arms of their concern, the men vacant and glittery

with spandex and oil. It is November, and already books thicken
at my bedside, a crush of paper characters awaiting the eye's

hurried pass, their unread stories attendant through the night,
until its bandage lifts to a morning blush, and I am held

within the parenthesis of a spare white house, a little thinner,
empty hands chilled like the faithful, offering myself to discipline's

cool machinery. I will stand on the pier, gesturing and cold.
I will open my mouth to your opening mouth.

II.

Peonies

In the yard, peonies burst their white hearts,
scalloped edges unfolding only for themselves.
Their simplicity, the blade of it, cuts the morning.

In this Brooklyn of yards haloed in razor wire
and laundry flapping like flags of surrender,
resin smoke drifting up to these windows,

traveled shadows from a smoker's lungs,
I watch the police helicopter menace the neighborhood,
its engine hooking together manifold locks

and keys. Even now, in the face of this sickening,
there is forward movement, American needs
forcing my hand, each day a dull pearl

strung on a weakening line. The last time I saw you,
I held my hand over you while you slept, imagining heat
rising in green and red, as in a photograph of heat,

your body giving up its one treasure. There
is such savagery in this neglect—muscle strain,
fluid failure, the flesh receding

from bone until we are left with the indelible
print and fracture, our cells snapping
in a survivor's brain like grainy pictures,

the only way we'll last. I brought you peonies—
pink, like a shell, like a heaven, a mouth,
an infant, an infinity, a crisis, an end.

To Sleep in a New City

This is medicine's hollow miracle—that we have come to trust it.
So intent is the doctor, what he knows is to be envied.

Tell me, when did the pain start?
What I like most is how clean the room is, all the drawers

sliding smoothly, the heavy curtains gray as ash,
the corners of the floor sloping so even the smallest particle

can be swept away. In dreams I've had, birds flutter
and chop their wings like flames, a moon crests pale

as a dinner plate, and I drive out of this place
which is black and crumbled and lit with vacant specks.

Behind me in the mirror is an urban glow, huge and cumulative,
a match lit that will end it all, a globe of breath blowing smoke.

What I drive toward is a new city, one in which your body
does not wait for me, and this road dividing the night in half,

the trust I've put in oily machinery, this doctor's puzzling,
assures me the world does not pause for us.

The Bruise of This

The night I woke to find the sheets wet from you,
like a man cast up on the beach,
I hurried you off to the shower to cool you down,

dressed you, the garments strict and awkward in my hands,
and got you into a taxi to the hospital,
the driver eyeing us from his rearview mirror—

The blue tone of the paging bell,
the green smocks, metal beds,
plastic chairs linked

in a childhood diagram of infection,
and when they wheeled you by
there was a needle in your arm,

the bruise of this
already showing itself,
and rather than watch gloved doctors handle you

in their startling white coats and loose ties,
I took a seat outside and waited,
time yawning, thick and static—

and made clear to me in the bright light of speculation
was time's obstacle in the body,
and those things I could do that might cushion it.

On Opening

Look at it, the season's shifting.
I can see it from this slice of window—
fires smoldering on the hillside
and smoke rising up in feeble questions.

A dark house in the distance ignites
its one tinny light
and I think of light and the way
it can come too close like an enemy

or ice. Outside the wind sings
the way a door sings on opening,
and all day the hammer tap
in the next room is a heartbeat

sealing in the blood then giving in,
hungry for zero. I must tell you how willingly
the body will empty itself of itself.
Cancer coils in a distant cell,

blue veins snake to a quieter place
while the night's single white sheet
stretches out wrinkle-less, chilled,
the snow fields hoarding

their empty white bowls.
Listen to that whispering!
It is the lungs casting in and out—
a spidery black spot clings to pink.

How I Was Told and Not Told

There was the milky sun washing out the sky
and his hair fanned out on the pillow above
the drunk and muscled crush of him.

In the room, the night had left its mark—
ashes in a saucer, burning amber in a glass,
the slow ribbon of news slipping out.

The husk of his voice hangs
in the morning air, and outside
the wind starts its hurling.

Left lingering, a fossil,
is the shape of him
in the empty bed.

The needle punctures the vein
to consider the blood. No trace left
of the body's perfect red moon.

I am alarmed by the weight of objects
and the way light is consumed
by the greedy sky. In sleep

I have already heard the ruffling of papers,
the dry movements of insects,
the tray of utensils' bright

clatter and chime.
I lay down my want of him
like a lock of hair in a cedar box

and the moon with its bone sliver
and loose stitches of black
bastes up the night sky.

Thirst

In the painting above your bed a woman pauses,
lifts her arms upward in a gesture of infinite reticence,
protesting winds that are stagnant and a ship that won't move.

Why do you study me like this? While snowy pullets in the yard
    flare up
into white fires, you roost there, a jewel at the throat, a sad thing.
I stare down at your body's wreckage,

a field gleaned for its small nourishment, while the sun through
    the window
recoils its tail of far heat. I am no clean numeral. No simple boy.
You ask for a glass of ice, for water turned cold hardened water.

Winter of Heaven, Winter of Ash

The Visit Home

It is not yet light in Wisconsin.
The day's seven pale hours bow in the distance,
the sky an upturned bowl.

From the window, I see where a deer
has pawed through snow for apples
buried deep under a crust of ice.

Downstairs, Father rattles the coffee pot
while the television flickers with war in Yugoslavia.
A woman with a bundle. A tank cutting through snow.

At the cathedral, lights flicker in red cups
underneath a gold leaf icon. Lips move, but no prayers are said.
There is the smell of tobacco smoke, frankincense, cooking grease,

of hope gone out, of ice.

The Dream

DNA spirals upward
linking its bloody promise
to the cell's failure.
A friend begs
                    Take care of me.
while I walk the street,
a narrow chamber,
my pace like a ventricle
flapped open then shut.
I scour the filthy sky
for a route, a hole
I could slip
my self through
like a bone sliver.

In Brooklyn

When I try to concentrate, I see only details:
snow coating the guy wires linking house to house,
the way the old woman on the street folds and refolds
a slip of paper fluttering in her hands.
Is it a list?

A diagnosis?
Glass shatters in the alley
while the blue clock in the kitchen begins to buzz.
The noise is clutter's loose sister
and rises up around me like someone else's life.

My mother sends articles clipped from the home newspaper: *Rare Albino Deer Killed On Canada Ridge. Viola Wendt Dead at 72.* I'm making lists: sounds I would never miss (1) Glass breaking in the alley. (2) Merengue through the floorboards. I peer into the mirror at my face and its cluster of bones. (3) The squeal of the medicine cabinet door and the dull click of its magnet.

I have been given a bag of clothing, given to me because his family could not keep the lingering shapes of a dead son.

To say it happened by accident is to deny its significance. We had spent the afternoon putting on mud masks, plucking stray hairs, buffing our skin, manicures, the bathroom bright as day, and when he stepped into the shower with me, I could only notice the way water pooled in the pocket of his collarbone and slicked the fine blond hairs in a V down his back.

It has begun to snow.
I can no longer see out my window
nor down the tight angle of the street
that empties into the water.
A snowplow cuts a path, scraping by,

I put on a jacket that will never be my own.
The answering machine picks up a call from my mother,
Honey are you there? Please pick up the phone.
A candle near the window.
The acrid smell of a match gone out.

Wind bumps against the pane,
blue afternoon shadows lengthen.
In my dream there is no one I can answer.
There are too many sounds I would miss.

Elegy

Of the delicate pocket of his collarbone
where water pooled,
and dim crescents under his eyes.
Fine blond hairs,
the channel of his forearm,
muscle, and bone and semen,
a day marked off with clouds
blunt as horses.
Shadows lengthening blue on snow,
and sleep's impress
in the empty bed.
Confusion and pity
and the telephone's dark click
as the receiver is hung
on its rest.

The Mare

It's a miracle—
the steam draught from her nostrils,
muscle and sinew and bone,

and in the winter meadow
I turn. Over my shoulder
are the four overlapping prints

from her even stride. The deer
have left predawn tracks
simple as hunger

and unreadable.
Their silhouettes hang
ghostly against cedars.

Fugitive. Curl of smoke,
distant highway. A saw
whirling and biting the wood,

a pine arm waves under white.
I am moving away.
The mare is ignorant

and humors me. If this
is meant to be the end
I ask only to hear it

before I shift under its weight
and lean shadow,
or learn

to enter confusion
or pity, and make there
a place to live.

Pale Notion

I'm learning about paring down.
My one tin constellation.
My handful of keys to let you into places.

And this the palest of notions—
God's white underbelly hurtling like a planet,
a brush filling with your lightest hair

to be got rid of. Not the floor's
graceless shine beaming.
Not the windows' lie of bright air.

But the book creased shut
and the rumpled workers
all gone home.

In the Winter of This Climate

When I dream it is of sheep
tangled in the marsh, their calls
growing faint and the light failing

or winter's handful of piano notes
against the highway's salt hiss.
Nothing stays at home forever.

There is the house I go back to,
long since torn down,
and your footsteps walking the same five rooms

the day the men were frozen in their boats
when the weather changed
and a storm blew in from the east.

There is the sky filling with its same dim stars,
the night birds fanning in the tree's icy ribs
and you knee-deep in the river's motion

hand cupped to your head
an upturned palm filling with rapid blood,
your voice loose of its tether, saying

Do you hear it? Do you hear what I'm trying to say?

One Explanation of Beauty

Everywhere the material world is speaking to me—
the cry of a door or the floorboard's groan
with the slightest pressure of a foot,

or the pear tree blooming on the Avenue,
its cells bursting and multiplying,
the kindest thing I know. Here in this world capital

a new version of beauty reveals itself—
one of action, and people
shedding their lives like skins—a fury

recalcitrant as an animal circling its bed,
too stubborn to go down. In my heart,
its dumb fist pounding in me now,

I know what you are saying—that calm and stasis
are beautiful, like horses
with their platters of muscle and wet eyes.

That inactivity offers a window to look through
without opening, and permission to touch no thing.
That an image of a city is better than the city

itself, with its crude happenings and pain.
My choice has been made, for this
immeasurable velocity—because images burn,

and lives like ours
shatter like houses in a desperate wind—
But here, I leave you with this

because I know you will love it—a horse,
her bowed neck white and rippled
picking through wet grass, toward a looming grove.

Aubade

Again I've been searching for omens flimsy as they are, and the cat
who crossed my small yard, mornings, was the easiest.

Not my dreams, certainly—last night's scene of endless roller-
    blading
speeding at a velocity it's not difficult to imagine as erotic,

and fading this morning like the cologne of someone who's just left
the room. And when I turned over the letter you'd sent and I'd lost
    months ago

it was as if I'd just heard the lock click as you left for the morning,
my own day clear and solitary, waiting for your return. I think of
    the body's

imprecision, the dull tongs of your legs, the unasked question
of each upturned palm, how over coffee I'd noticed first your
    hands,

gripping a newspaper between forefinger and thumb
then your eyes hurrying on to the next word, the next period.

It's night here. The cat hasn't been seen for days, and I pretend
not to notice. Pretend I'll tell you when he fails to come home.

III.

Unmade Bed

You remember the billboard of the unmade bed on Lafayette and Fourth? It's finally down. It peeled and faded and last week they took it down. The city changes like that, after so much of the same. Things get erased or gone over again.

Three days ago I read about these men who steal cows—curious. They don't take them alive, but bring a truck into the pasture and slaughter the beasts right out in the open, in the middle of the night. They pack the meat, cut in rough shapes, and leave the hides and innards, bones, for dogs to scrap over and haul to dusty yards. Farmers wake and find nothing left, their fences cut wide open, a gaped mouth in the morning, the field empty.

Went shopping with C. and spent an hour finding her lipstick. It was so important, just the right shade, you know? We kept smearing them on the backs of our hands, little cosmetic bruises, turning each tongue down its silver throat, dozens, each wrong. I have this tissue with her lip print, perfect *Russian Sable,* not too much brown, though not garish, and I've promised to buy her several if I ever find a match.

And me thinking of the panels of your body pinning me down, your hair. I haven't had it that good since. I saw a doctor. There was a lecture I could have done without, and I'm fine, so don't worry. When they took the blood and I saw the three vials on the counter, little jewels, so red—I could almost see the cells colliding, a galaxy. Forgive me. There will be more mornings, waking alone, when a print of me in the bed is laundered and pinned on a line, is gone.

Chapel of the Miraculous Medal

C. calls to tell me Mercury is in retrograde, so watch out. Just last night, walking up the subway stairs at Fourteenth Street, some guy reaches under her skirt and grabs her. *You see? The whole city is nuts. Who was that guy? What a freak!* she says.

And that old apartment in Chicago, three rickety stories up, the man across the street baring himself to me every morning at 7, and again evenings at 6:30, waiting for my light to go on; his glassed-in want a naked torso behind the window. I never saw his face, just the activity, not even distance or geography could prevent him from gesturing.

In Paris there is a convent on the rue du Bac where the body of a saint lies under glass, resisting decay for a century. The nun stubbornly holds on to form, waxy hands clasped over her heart, an insect in amber.

I can barely write this to you. There was a boy. At a bar, he spoke to me, so young, mistaking me for someone younger, and groping him in the corner, his soft mouth on mine, I swear I'd forgotten how it could be, so necessary. I left him there, whispered in his ear, and hurried back to my empty rooms.

I was walking along the piers, all the men on roller blades, the orange sun dipping down orange-red into New Jersey, and I was back in the attic room I rented from—Rose, that was her name, calling upstairs to ask if I'd like a tomato. She must have had an extra from the garden, and when I opened the door an hour or so later, it was nested in my shoe. Red, as big as my fist, one perfect thing left there just for me.

Fourteen Things We're Allowed to Bring to the Underworld

Did you get the photo I sent? The horse? I would take her with me. I used to go to her stall and just press my ear against that swimming belly, the liquid of her. I could sleep lying atop that animal, all iron smell, shifting from foot to foot. All hay.

What would you take? What things? L. says Fire, and I understand that, and would take that too. Architecture, fretwork for structure. The miniature tea set for delicacy. Opera for blood. Iron for fortitude and weight. Linen as a reminder of skin. Crystal for simple music. Tin. Leather for harnessing. Paper. Milk. A boat. I'll stop one short.

Ron Vawter is gone, I imagine you've heard. He was on an airplane, over the ocean when he was taken. Imagine, in flight. Remember it, the Soho garage where we saw him, reclined on the dais, draping himself in strings of beads and wrapping his head in a silver turban, the turban's refusal. He was thin, I was shocked by that, and the lesion bloomed on the patch of his leg we weren't meant to see.

Give me this one thing. Summer is impossible, you must understand. I cannot survive there, that house. All day the muddy river pushes by, and you there watching it.

Predictions about a Black Car

Four boys have been arrested for killing geese. This is how it happened: The first pinned back the white-pinioned wings. The second stretched the neck, held shut the damaged and rubbery bill. The third bit through feather and esophagus, his mouth filled with its blood. The last boy kept the other geese herded in the corner, watched. I do not know what will become of them, though the town hopes for something extravagant.

By now I know you've heard of my accident—the black car stopped in front of me, my dramatic spin to the ditch. You were there when the psychic warned me about such a car, before she rubbed her hands with alcohol and set her palms ablaze. At the hospital they x-rayed my wrist, its club and piston flaring into the hand's calcium branch, the flesh translucent and ashy, an undersea picture.

I've been reading a book about a storm, folded into thirds, twisting its way north with a tropical fury. In it, the fishing boat, a moveable target, is pitched against the waves until its light is finally doused, hull pulled apart, another story with property at its center.

There was a morning this spring when the sky was washed of any choler. I could hear the ocean from my small yard, breathing in and out. Two gulls cried from their perch near the chimney. You weren't here, and I'm sorry for that; my heart was quiet, in need of no other.

No Place Like Home

On the Kansas highway I see children being useful, driving cars. Twelve or thirteen years old, boys mostly, peering over dashboards in pickups with rusted wheel wells and gravel on the floor. At a stop sign in Hays I catch myself staring at the tanned bare arm hanging out of a truck window. We are landlocked. The sky stretching out above us is huge and useless. I look up at this boy, at his brown face and wheat-blond head, and my heart catches and I panic.

In rest stops all across America, men wait in cars for sex to happen to them, the burning cities of their radios glowing, the voices ringing out like instructions for a new route home. There is that altitude that happens after sex, a heady chime like crystal, and thumbing their vinyl steering wheels I imagine the men hear it too. I have stopped to read the graffiti on the bathroom's beetle-colored walls. A crude phallus points the way to an empty stall, and dates tell of dozens of afternoons spent parked under a low tree's blunt canopy, eyes peeled on the soda machine, waiting for no one.

When did it all begin? I spend the evening staring out the motel window, a man gone thin and unhappy with diligence, my fear at this place generous. At the grocery the woman at the check-out smiles and I see something familiar in the way her grin pulls at her eyes, slipping my carton of milk in a bag and handing it over, a secret between just her and me. I pay and walk outside, gun the engine, drive out on the empty strip.

This is America—beetles clustered with the harvest, dust roads trundling off at perfect angles, and signs proclaiming unbearable roadside attractions.

Letter Written to a Verse by Karen Carpenter

The sky had been clear all day—so clear with a high wind, and when the sun began to sink, it was stained a liquid red. Yes, I know, it's pollution that gives it color—the light reflected off soot suspended in air.

I've been listening to the Carpenters—I know that will make you laugh, but I just keep thinking about Karen warding off the world by paring her body down. Nights when I can't sleep, I rewind the tape and listen to the tiny backward spiral of her voice, perfect pitch the only thing to last.

I think I will forgive you for not telling me, but for now that's not possible. Some mornings I imagine you getting on the bus and sitting by me and I hold your hand. We'd sit there facing forward and watch the city rushing in at us, like history's weight or a comet.

Got a postcard from L. with a photo of The Great Sphinx of Giza, mailed from Chicago, and I knew reading her looped words, that I'd never see it, and that meant nothing to me. Despite its magnitude and weighty decision, it's a moveable thing.

All That, Stammering

In the orchard at the edge of the ragged pines, the apples come thundering down and the deer turn over the darkening fruit. This is where I imagine you going. A place thick with beneficial insects and greening.

You have said it is possible to see shapes flickering around people, now that your eyes have found a new function, now that the weather has changed, now that I've gone. I ask what you see around me. *Red wings* you say.

You know what, you can take it back. I have no interest. I'm just not interested in this part. *Tell me about the ice skating,* you say, and I shake my head and you say *Tell.* So, I say, it was on the lake, up North. Just ice like a sheet of glass, like a window looked through, but dark. And at night, the cold went down deep and it moaned. The ice cracked and it moaned.

In a story I've been tending, I hear girls singing and there's a pasture full of sheep, and I have a giant mastiff to help me. The sheep escape and tangle in the marsh and their fear of the dog makes them scatter. I call and call, they go farther away, and it's too dark to see. I stir, and rain is falling in long gray blades. I fall back asleep and now the sheep have calmed, they answer me and slip back through the fence. The singing stopped, did I say that? The singing stopped.

IV.

Suture

Someday I will leave this town and not look back
but for now I keep hurtling toward
the red center, the road unfolding,

the ice raining down in crystals
while the bridge heaves itself onto the bank;
river of mud, river of sad oily pleasures

where a kingfisher cuts through the water's brown skin
clean as math, and I want to say
this is like logic, but something fails me.

Listen to the unforgivable birds
piercing cold sky and singing like needle and thread
and feel for the scar splitting my eyebrow.

(You remember the doctor tying his knots, don't you?)
This is always mine—the shadow of an animal,
smell of newly shorn wool, the workhorse pawing air

and stomping in his stall. Somewhere in the marsh
cress sharpens green in this age of stunted miracles.
But how to get there from here?

Hunt

The doe hanging stiff in the farmyard
is no mistake—her ribs splayed
and the kitchen sputtering.
Don't let me hear your voice waver.

The sky's bandage tangles in the trees
and dogs howl at dry stars and imagined
bodies—two stories below
the animal goes on dying.

The wind turns a secret over
in its big empty mouth
and in this bed I turn and touch
my shorn scalp

as if I were some new person.
Yesterday a deer clattered onto the road.
Her neck, the brittle way
she had of moving reminded me

how clumsy the world is.
In the morning, my father and brother
will go into the woods,
the smell of blood returning with them,

their faces changed.
I will stand in the window
with my face turned out
swallowing this particular taste for it.

The Shot

Duluth 1929

In her lap, the woman holds a gun.
The harbor bells ply one watery note
and behind them, the river road strings
through jack pine, scrub oak,
a ragged ornament of raven flapping

in a crude line north. She waits
inside the car, her finger nervously
skirting the trigger. Each ship's
blinding eye of light, Lake Superior's
wash and retreat, a heel tapping

a paving stone near the car—
none of it clarifies this moment.
For the woman, there is only the night
blackening around her, her fear
and the gun.

> the thin knife,
> the glittering fish scale
> the diamond earring
> the almond-shaped thumbnail
> the crease on the palm
> the scar from the dog bite
> the scar from the oven
> the penny in the shoe
> the twist of cigarette smoke
> the hand's blue veins
> the voice's appeal

Under dim light
in back of the house
the woman stands
pinning laundry to the line.
The garments are rough outlines
of bodies disassembled.
They are familiar

as is the river
pushing its watery load south
past this town,
the beach rough like a suture
and smelling of mud and of fish.

And because she knows comfort
can be found in diligence
she folds the dry clothes
smelling of grass, or clean water,
and because this repetition is like love
she pins up the wash, and repeats
what she knows by heart.

Spring, and the brown water
rises up, seeping into basements,
mud drying in rings on the walls
marking those years when the water
could not be held back
and when dried and gone, shows a place
that had once been filled.

1932

The space a person once occupied, the vacancy vibrant, space wanting to be filled, sound entering, a sudden clap, a delicate ringing in the ear.

She picks up her son at school. The 22's are in the car, shells in the pockets of her apron, and they drive out to the city dump where they shoot rats—the mounds of garbage alive with them. At first they are difficult to see—one must have an eye for details. Three creep out from underneath the rubble, spilling across the metal cage of a mattress. Shoot, reload, don't hesitate—small bodies marked with the bead—reload, fire again.

Greasy smell of burning garbage, faint hot blood pooling and thickening, the clap and echo, the gun's chilled report, an answer.

1929

The woman and man ride together in a car.
The sun they speed toward is yellow-tipped,
sprawling. They do not speak. The hum
of tires against the road vibrates
in the air like something severed.

She twists the ring on her finger,
as if to tighten it,
while what has been done goes unsaid—
he tells her nothing.
Opening out before them

is the river's loose string of prairie islands,
the isolated cottonwood and hawthorn
stripped down, branches splaying like a ribcage.
They both know what has been broken
is too large and will never properly mend.

    the click of the trigger
    the smoke in the chamber
    the bead on the target
    the report and echo
    the barrel's oily sheen
    the kick from the discharge
    the body's slight movement
    the bruise on the shoulder
    the knocking of the heart

1993

In the photo I have, all three kneel,
birds fanned out before them in the grass—
a good day. Two retrievers pant
over the kill. The woman tilts her head—
out of the sun? To hide the scar?
The man's cigarette smolders, smoke frozen

on paper. The boy looks into the camera's
blind eye, a smooth face, a loose grin,
his Winchester across one bent knee—
he is so confident that their suffering
cannot touch him anymore, 18 years old
and on his way out.

> the scar splitting my eyebrow
> the scar at my lip
> the hand on my arm
> the river slipping its banks
> the water and its debris
> the target and its splinters
> the shot and its vibrations
> the gun's weight in my hands
> the question and its answer

In the sky, a dimness hangs like a weight,
the sun, its perfect counterpoint. It is early.
Father is loading the gun.
He slips each shell into the chamber
until he hears the interior click of each deposit.

My body knows no other tension like this.
The damp air loosens my grip of the gun
and sweat trickles down my temple.
I look at Father's hand, its muscles and veins,
recount its grip on my arm. *Pull*

The clay target sails out, stiff, artificial,
Father shoots and splinters shower down. *Pull*
Another. The blast vibrates in my ears,
his body jerks, his weight absorbing the shock.
I step up to the line,

a taste bitter in my mouth.
I trace the scar on my brow,
sense failure moving in toward me,
my cheek pressing lightly against wood, metal.
In the sky, bruise-colored clouds glide past, *Pull*

The target, released, arcs out. I miss. *Pull*
Trigger click, hesitation before the blast,
shrill sound like a voice, fractured second
a lifetime, a shot.

This Heat, These Human Forms

Two years ago, while crossing the street, a group of boys came toward me. One grabbed me around the neck from behind, another punched me, twice, quickly in the face. I felt embarrassed. A third blow hit me squarely in the eye, and rage climbed on me like an animal. I twisted by the elbow the boy who held me, forced him to the ground, pinned him with my knees before breaking his jaw with my fist. He did not get up. The others helped him up.

The stars shone down, while the moon rose up out of the bay.
And there was your face, come to me from the dead.

The summer I turned sixteen I rode a school bus two hundred miles to an abandoned medical school on the edge of a small state college. Badger Boys State—mock government. I endured the compulsory sports, the scooping chain-link bunks, patriotic music blaring at lunch time. The state coroner came to show us slides—a cautionary tale—of the worst deaths he'd witnessed—men twisted into the power take-offs of tractors, a whole family overtaken by silo gas and fallen to their deaths while attempting rescue. And then the man who, bereft, locked himself in his bathroom with cases of beer and drank until it took him down so far he'd never cross back.

I imagine the shapes your feet would make in wet sand,
your hand cold at the back of my neck.

She spent her childhood in a Cuban institution, this psychic. It was hoped that through a strict schedule and medications, the visions she saw twisting through the world could be quelled. Seated in the doorway of a coat closet in a Vietnamese restaurant, the woman looked small, feeble. Above me she saw two hovering spirits, one of an infant, pink, aborted, the other an old man watching from my left shoulder. They were there to help, I was told. She warned me about liquor, a black car, the diseases of the throat, and finally rubbed her hands with oil and set them ablaze, pressed the flames into my upturned palm, extinguishing them there.

A day will come when I will walk, alone, down a city street, and not
   think of you,
the breathy shops gleaming, hurrying toward some unknown
   occasion.

At the street fair, four men stand on the yellow line dividing the street and crack their blacksnake bull whips. They wear black leather—chaps, chest harnesses, steel-toed boots. One wears rings and a chain from enlarged and distended nipples. They circle the whips overhead and crack them as a coachman might, with pleasure and seriousness for their vocation. They are positioned along the line so that the length of each cracking whip barely touches the man on either side.

No portentous birds today, no letter I could not manage to open.
Only a sky swept clean of what's been troubling me for weeks.

The knitting machines are sensitive, so the workers remove their ear plugs to better hear the mechanism unspool, to avoid malfunction. My job is to roll out the bolts of acrylic knit, trace the uniform pattern—armhole, bodice, sleeve, waistband— and cut the shapes with the spinning cutter's wheel, its finger-guard unscrewed for greater speed. At noon we sit on upturned pails at the loading dock, smoke exactly three cigarettes, speak loudly over the ringing in our ears.

I remember with gratitude the sight of your hand on the steering
   wheel,
the weight of the other resting lightly on my knee.

At fourteen, I bought a horse—the most beautiful animal I'd ever seen. Her gaits were so smooth she could be ridden bareback, at trot or gallop and never compromise the rider. Every day I would ride her through the paddock to a neighbor's pasture where the cedars opened onto a creek bed and meadow. I'd knot my hands in her mane and let her run, unhindered, the snaffle in her mouth unchecked.

Love, please. Don't.
It is difficult enough without your body in the world.

56

Difficult Body

A story: There was a cow in the road, struck by a semi—
half-moon of carcass and jutting legs, eyes
already milky with dust and snow, rolled upward

as if tired of this world tilted on its side.
We drove through the pink light of the police cruiser,
her broken flank blowing steam in the air.

Minutes later, a deer sprang onto the road
and we hit her, crushed her pelvis—the drama reversed,
first consequence, then action—but the doe,

not dead, pulled herself with front legs
into the ditch. My father went to her, stunned her
with a tire iron before cutting her throat, and today I think

of the body of St. Francis in the Arizona desert,
carved from wood and laid in his casket,
lovingly dressed in red and white satin

covered in petitions—medals, locks of hair,
photos of infants, his head lifted and stroked,
the grain of his brow kissed by the penitent.

O wooden saint, dry body. I will not be like you,
carapace. A chalky shell scooped of its life.
I will leave less than this behind me.